Fuzz and Buzz

Written by Caroline Green

Illustrated by Omar Aranda

Collins

Fuzz and Buzz zigzag.

Fuzz is quick.

They dash and zip.

Fuzz gets wet.

7

Fuzz hops on.

Buzz taps the rock.

Thud!

Fuzz gets on the rock.

Fuzz and Buzz sit and chat.

12

ZZ

14

After reading

Letters and Sounds: Phase 3

Word count: 40

Focus phonemes: /w/ /z/ zz /qu/ /ch/ /sh/ /th/ /nk/

Common exception words: and, they, the

Curriculum links: Understanding the world

Early learning goals: Reading: read and understand simple sentences; use phonic knowledge to decode regular words and read them aloud accurately; read some common irregular words

Developing fluency

- Your child may enjoy hearing you read the book.
- Take turns to read a page, with your child reading the right-hand pages. Discuss a suitable bee voice for the speech bubbles.

Phonic practice

- Focus on words in which two letters make one sound.
- Turn to pages 4 and 5. Point to **dash**, then **Rush** and **Buzz**, asking your child to sound out and blend each word. Ask: Which two letters in these words make the /sh/ and /z/ sounds? Turn to pages 12 and 13 and repeat for:

  thanks (*"th" and "nk"*)   Fuzz (*"zz"*)   Buzz (*"zz"*)   chat (*"ch"*)

- Look at the "I spy sounds" pages (14–15) together. Ask your child to describe what they can see. Next, take turns to find a word in the picture containing a "zz" or /sh/ sound. (e.g. *Fuzz, Buzz, puzzle; shark, ship, fish, bush, shells*)

Extending vocabulary

- Look at page 4. Ask your child:
  - Which words tell us they are flying fast? (*dash, zip*)
  - What other creatures might dash? (e.g. *rabbits, tigers*)
- Look at page 5 and talk about the meaning of the word **Rush**. (*hurry*) Ask:
  - What is the opposite of hurry? (e.g. *go slowly, crawl*)
  - What creatures might move along slowly? (e.g. *snails, tortoises*)